Giant water bugs
(fried or boiled
in ancient and modern
Southeast Asia)

Toxic shark meat
rotted till it's "edible"
(enjoyed in Iceland from
Viking times to today)

Squid ink
(swirled into sauces in
ancient and modern Europe,
Asia, and Africa)

Eel pie
(featured in English feasts
from ancient to modern
times—rat pie, too)

Goliath bird-eating spiders
(hand-caught and roasted over campfires
in prehistoric and modern Venezuela)

Witchetty grubs
(giant moth caterpillars
relished raw or roasted in
prehistoric and modern Australia)

Tuna eyeballs
(fried, boiled, or sautéed
in ancient and modern Japan)

Live stink bug tacos
(feast food in prehistoric and
modern Mexico)

Deep-fried starfish
(savored in ancient and
modern China)

Scorpions on sticks
(nibbled and munched
prehistoric and modern
Asia)

Jerky
(dried meat ranging from alligator
to beef to camel to zebra,
gnawed globally)

Banana and
dandelion leaf smoothies
(chugged today in the US)

Eat Your Woolly Mammoths!

Two Million Years of the World's Most Amazing Food Facts, from the Stone Age to the Future

Copyright © 2022 by James Solheim

All rights reserved. Manufactured in Italy.

For information address HarperCollins Children's Books, a division of HarperCollins Publishers,

195 Broadway, New York, NY 10007.

www.harpercollinschildrens.com

The art combines James Solheim's pencil drawings, digital drawings,
and photographs with images from around the world and outer space.
The text type is 14-point Typography of Coop, Forged.

Library of Congress Cataloging-in-Publication Data is available.

ISBN 978-0-06-239705-8 (hardcover)

22 23 24 25 26 RTLO 10 9 8 7 6 5 4 3 2 1

First Edition

 GREENWILLOW BOOKS

Eat Your Woolly Mammoths!

Two Million Years of the World's Most Amazing Food Facts, from the Stone Age to the Future

Words and Pictures by

JAMES SOLHEIM

Greenwillow Books
An Imprint of HarperCollins Publishers

CONTENTS

Eww, gross!

SIX TONS OF DELICIOUS

Even in the Stone Age, kids wanted what tasted good.

But they didn't have to settle for candy bars, ice cream, or cupcakes piled with rainbow sprinkles. They got to eat real food.

Lifting crackly, smoky meat to their lips, tasting burnt wood and blood in each slurp, they knew what kept them strong.

Chewy worms and crunchy bugs. Brains and livers and eyeballs. And best of all, fresh, hot woolly mammoths. Stone Age kids needed more than burgers to survive.

(To survive lunch, that is.)

Let the feast begin!

PART ONE

FOODS FROM PREHISTORY

THE DISCOVERY OF FROZEN DINNERS

Before the first ever grocery store, before the invention of the wheel, lunch meant a fight and a sore back. It meant conquering an animal much bigger than you or searching the hills for weeds that might be food or might be poison.

That was prehistory—before the invention of writing made knowing the distant past possible. In Mesopotamia (writing's birthplace), prehistory ended over five thousand years ago. In the rest of the world, it ended later.

But even without written history to help us, we still know much of what prehistoric people ate.

They ate woolly mammoths. They ate bugs and frogs and other wild delicacies. Scientists still find their leftovers, so we *know.* Even today, alert eyes sometimes discover whole woolly mammoths frozen in the earth, their meat edible after thousands of years.

An actual baby mammoth found frozen in Russia

Edible, yes. But when scientists made stew out of a 36,000-year-old bison, paleontologist Mary Lee Guthrie said it "tasted like mud." And when scientist Semyon Grigoryev tasted raw mammoth meat fresh from the ground, he complained that it was a little tough and hard.

COLD LUNCH

In *1991,* hikers found a prehistoric man sticking out of an Italian glacier. Over five thousand years ago, someone killed him with an arrow and he froze. He stayed frozen as fifty centuries came and went.

Scientists dug food out of his stomach to see what he ate in his last day of life.

He ate mountain goat meat, probably dried like jerky or bacon. He also ate goat fat, wheat, cancer-causing ferns, and part of a deer (maybe its organs, like its liver or brain). Plus prehistoric flies!

BACON BOY

Lemme outa here!

AUNTIE URGLE'S SPECIAL STEW

Our prehistoric ancestors didn't have toothbrushes. Fossil teeth over a million years old are still clumped with fossilized crust. In this crust, scientists found fibers of raw meat, a flake of a butterfly wing, part of an insect leg, wood, and—oh, no!—vegetables.

THE WORLD'S OLDEST RHINO BLOOD

The idea seemed impossible, but it worked. Scientists led by human-origins expert April Nowell tested stone knives for traces of prehistoric meat—and found it.

After 250,000 years buried in the desert of Jordan, three knives still had dried blood in their cracks. Tests for rhinoceros proteins proved it was rhino blood. Other stone tools nearby had been used on meat from horses, camels, ducks, wild cattle, and elephants.

Rhino knife, actual size

In 1976, a class at George Stevens Academy in Maine saved a Twinkie to see how long it would last. Now it is the world's oldest. Will it survive as long as rhino blood on a stone blade?

A little lower
and to the left.
Yessssss. . . .
Ahhhh. . . .

History-making Twinkie,
actual size

3

DON'T EAT THE RHINOCERI

Mammoths weren't the only woolly ones. Rhinos were often woolly, too, and like the mammoths, woolly rhinos are now extinct—maybe from being overhunted.

Today's rhinos are almost extinct, just like their woolly ancestors. They're in danger because some people eat ground-up rhino horns, believing the powder cures cancer and solves other health problems.

But rhino horns are actually made of the same protein as fingernails and horse hooves. Eating rhino horns is like eating fingernails in hoof sauce.

So be a friend to the rhinos! Don't eat their horns.

ABOUT TWO MILLION YEARS AGO

somebody ate hippos, rhinos, crocodiles, turtles, zebras, bone marrow, antelope brains, and wildebeest brains.

The earliest food clues in the human story are about meat. That's because prehistory's eager eaters hacked at their food with stone tools that left cut marks on the bones. Judging from the high number of busted skulls, diners especially enjoyed the nutritious brains.

700,000 YEARS AGO

somebody ate a rhino's meat and bone marrow—and probably turtles, a giant lizard, and a stegadon (related to elephants).

In a cave in the Philippines, scientists found scratched rhino bones buried next to stone scrapers that matched the scratches. These bones from about 700,000 years ago give clear evidence of our human ancestors scraping off meat for their food.

THEY PROBABLY ATE THE RHINO RAW.

The bones show no signs of burning or heating. Most evidence of humans cooking appears hundreds of thousands of years later.

Frostee Brain

I don't *care* whether cooking has been invented yet. I'm not gonna eat my rhino raw.

THE PERFECT PARTY SNACK: INSECTS

Even the youngest Stone Age child could catch a grasshopper or cricket. And visitors often brought snacks: lice and fleas. Bugs on the body were a natural part of life that provided friends with togetherness and nutrition.

Prehistoric people ate

termites

crickets

fleas

beetles

caterpillars

random green things with too many eyes

lice

cockroaches

ants

grasshoppers

houseflies

In the tradition of the ancestral geniuses who tamed fire and invented tools and underwear, scientist Albert Einstein once gobbled a fresh, raw grasshopper he found in the grass, according to his driver. The omega-3 fatty acids in insects help humans grow healthy brains such as this one.

6

GREAT DISCOVERIES OF SCIENCE

Scientists have studied the places that ancient people used for toilets, and found lots to pick apart. Termite body parts made up more than three-fourths of one prehistoric person's contribution to science, left nearly ten thousand years ago.

Careful study of other specimens came up with chewed ticks, a louse, and an abundance of grasshoppers.

One person even ate a whole rattlesnake, including a fang.

Skeet's Discovery Service

One-Hour Science Discoveries Guaranteed

78% Termites   22% Other

A SCRUMPTIOUS STINK

In parts of Mexico, tacos stuffed with living, twitching stink bugs are a healthy tradition going back centuries. The city of Taxco celebrates this heritage in yearly stink bug feasts. Rich in protein, vitamins, and cinnamon-apple flavor, stink bugs are more than just a treat.

My taco tickled me!

The kids at school don't call us stinkers.

They like us so much they eat us!

Get back in me, you little stinkers!

7

Did cave moms make their kids conquer the saber-toothed giant brussels sprout?

DID CAVE KIDS EAT THEIR BROCCOLI?

In prehistoric times, there was no such thing as broccoli. Not only did Stone Age kids miss out on ice cream, they even had to live without broccoli and brussels sprouts.

Over the centuries, the world's farmers developed all of today's main vegetables from wild plants. Amazingly, scientists still find bits of their untamed prehistoric vegetables on Stone Age grinding tools.

Preshistoric kids ate

moonwort root flour

cattails

smartweed

cacti

Aw, Mom, can't I have some raw turtle guts?

Not until you finish your moonwort burger, Missy.

GUT HUT

TOTOPOCA!

Corn started out as a weed. Visionary farmers in Mexico planted some of their biggest and tastiest kernels each year as seeds instead of eating them, and over the centuries, corn inherited those seeds' size and flavor. Corn became a yummy giant that barely looks like its ancestor.

The Incas often paired their corn with a plump, nutritious guinea pig.

PREHISTORY'S FINEST FRESH POP-CORN 6000 YEARS OLD

Teosinte: corn's weed ancestor, actual size

Popcorn cob over six thousand years old found in Peru, actual size

Corn today is a sophisticated product of more than nine thousand years of cultivation and breeding, resulting in its inimitable good taste.

Ancient farmers developed broccoli, brussels sprouts, cabbage, cauliflower, and kale all from one type of plant, a flowering wild mustard.

Aunt of Frankenweed

This book is scary!

Don't worry. Grandpa was a weed, too, and he never hurt a pea.

DID CAVE KIDS CHEW GUM?

Used chewing gum speckles the planet. Scientists have found many wads that are thousands of years old, with tooth prints so defined you can see the chewers' cavities. Most of the clearest prints came from children between the ages of five and fifteen. A child's first set of teeth are different from adult teeth, so it's possible to identify some gum chewers as six or younger.

Scientists could tell from DNA molecules in the gum what the chewers ate and even some details of what they looked like.

Gum chewed about ten thousand years ago in Sweden by a boy around twelve to fourteen years old.

About five thousand years old, discovered by a student helping scientists dig for prehistoric artifacts in Finland.

Birch-bark tar gum about 5,700 years old from Denmark, chewed by a blue-eyed girl with dark hair and dark skin, who ate eels and duck meat.

GUM BITES

Native people of Maine and eastern Canada chewed sap from spruce trees and waterproofed their canoes with it. Lumberjacks carved book-shaped wooden boxes and sent spruce gum to their sweethearts in them.

INNOVATORS OF THE GUM WORLD

More than five hundred years ago, Aztec women in Mexico and Guatemala developed a high-tech chewing gum that lasted longer, didn't crumble, and stayed softer than the traditional gums of the time.

They made it from natural rubber mixed with bitumen, used today to make asphalt roads. They added *axin* to soften the final product.

Axin was a yellow, oily chemical that bubbled out of an inch-long bug called an aje, or axe, when it was cooked.

BUY!
PURCHASE!
ACQUIRE!

All Natural . . .

Quetzalxochitl's Bug Tar Gum

Mastic gum from the Greek island of Chios—so valued that Chios turned its towns into forts to fend off pirates.

Ptooey!

Hey, the ancient Greeks are supposed to attack on somebody else's page!

PART TWO

THE BRONZE AND IRON AGES

ANCIENT EGYPT
About 3300 BC to 31 BC

Unfair! You left out us Mesopotamians! Our foods were humdingers, too!

WHAT WOULD A MUMMY WANT FOR LUNCH?

Mummified meat, of course!

Ancient Egyptians believed that the dead would wake up hungry, so they stocked their tombs with plenty of goodies. Just a few of the mummified foods in mummy lunchboxes included cooked ducks, geese, kidneys, livers, gizzards, cow tail soup, pigeon pie, and pieces of sheep, cows, and goats.

Um . . . thanks, but Tut's celebrating his five thousandth, and I'm invited!

If you eat your mummies like a good boy, that dessert over there is for you.

I'LL PAY YOU IN GUM!

The ancients used sap from the mastic tree for chewing gum, spice, and medicine—when they could afford it. Its price sometimes reached gold's. Egypt used it to make mummies—especially the tasty food mummies for their afterlife feasts. Chew it, cook with it, stir it into mummy varnish to keep your pharaohs shiny and fresh!

MUMMY MEDICINE

Starting about eight hundred years ago, Europe's doctors gave their patients *mumia*—ground-up human mummies—to eat as cures for everything from headaches to seizures.

One of today's biggest drug companies (the Merck Group) still offered mumia in 1909 as "genuine Egyptian mummy—while supplies last"—and sold it in 1924 by the kilogram.

Hey! Give me back my corpse!

OPEN 24 HOURS

EXIT ONLY

MUMIA

When ancient Egyptians got sick, the food got wild. They fed whole cooked mice to sick children. They treated a stomachache with a crushed hog's tooth in cake. Got any problems with arms or legs? The cure was to eat scrapings of a statue!

IS DELIVERY INCLUDED?

John Sanderson, a London merchant, wrote in 1586 about his part in the medicinal mummy trade. He said that after being lowered on ropes into a mummy mine, he broke off parts and "brought home divers [diverse] heads, hands, armes [arms] and feet."

He delivered six hundred pounds of mummy for England's Turkey Company "in pieces" and gave a mummy's hand to his brother.

Today the Merck Group in Germany has two mummy heads on display, reminders of the company's days as a mumia seller.

MOLE RATS THAT SATISFY

The oldest collections of writings ever found come from Mesopotamia. Thanks to the region's love of writing, we know the Mesopotamians right down to their grocery lists and to the pickled grasshopper sauce that gave much of their cooking its zing.

King Ashurnasirpal II* bragged on a stone monument about the foods he served at a feast—listing ten thousand sheep, five hundred gazelles, ten thousand doves, and thousands of other foods.

I ordered TEN THOUSAND jumping mice, not 9,999.

Nobody's comin' to OUR feast and not gettin' a dead mouse with all the fixin's.

*This king was a precision braggart who claimed he served ten thousand jumping mice at a feast that had 69,574 guests. "Jumping mice" are called jerboas today. They can jump three to six feet straight up!

BE GENEROUS WiTH YOUR MOLE RATS

Mole rats are so yummy that the Mesopotamians saw them as a special food for kings and priests.

Tutu-magir sent me seven mole rats ... I kept just one to eat myself, and it tasted excellent! Had I known how good they were, I'd not have sent a single one to the temple official! Now, as to why I'm writing: When you go down to Tur-Ugalla, tell the orchard keeper who lives there he should dig up fifteen mole rats for me and send them here.

—from an ancient letter imprinted into a clay tablet

O great King Hammurabi, I bring thee a mole rat with extra cheese as tribute to thy somber nobility, grandeur, and wisdom.

PARTY TIIIME!

THIS SOUP TASTES LIKE SOME ANIMAL'S SPLEEN

With a few words still undeciphered, translators have figured out enough to cook up some tasty dishes from the world's oldest known recipes. (The spleen is an organ that filters an animal's blood.)

Enjoy!

SPLEEN AND STOMACH SOUP
A Mesopotamian recipe from about 1800 BC

Get some water ready. Add fat. Toss in pieces of salted stomach and spleen along with milk. Add crushed *kasû* [a type of spice or wild licorice], cake crumbs, and [a word that hasn't been decoded]. Add salt, onion, flour, [another unknown word], roasted dough, top-quality mint, and mashed leeks and onions. Thicken with blood. It is ready to serve.

Hundreds of thousands of clay tablets preserved the Mesopotamians' writings. This side of a clay tablet shows seven recipes.

LOOKING YOUNG WITH THE ANCIENT GREEKS

Most Greeks ate ordinary things like bread, fruit, and fish. But Greece was also the land of celebrities—athletes, authors, actors, and teachers with ideas for special diets.

THE PYTHAGOREAN DIET

For centuries, vegetarians called themselves Pythagoreans because the Greek thinker Pythagoras was the first famous person to avoid eating animals.

He also believed that babies' souls lived in fava beans before birth. Legend says he died when he refused to flee into a bean field while being chased by his enemies.

> Eat only fruit, nuts, grains, honey, and milk.

> No beans! Stop hurting poor, innocent beans!

A SELECTION OF ARCHESTRATUS'S SPECIALTIES

Moray eels

Conger eels

Fat eels

Thin eels

Tender eels

Eel heads

Sea anemones

Electric rays

Octopi

Squid

AND YUCK! TUNA FISH!

ARCHESTRATUS

The world's first celebrity gourmet wrote *The Life of Luxury*, the book that set the standard for tasteful cooking.

> Keep food simple.

> Use fresh and local ingredients.

> Let the honest flavor of a fat eel or fresh squid shine through.

MILO'S OLYMPIAN DIET

Ancient Greece invented the Olympics, and Milo of Croton was its first mega-star. The world's greatest athlete from about 536 to 520 BC, he became the subject of wild stories and exaggerated health claims.

His fabled workout and diet would kill anyone who actually tried it.

❯ Eat twenty pounds of meat daily.

❯ Eat twenty pounds of bread daily.

❯ Drink two and a half gallons of wine daily.

❯ Eat stones found in rooster gizzards.

❯ Carry a growing bull every day for four years, then eat the whole bull in one day (at least six hundred pounds, and probably a lot more).

Milo's daily diet would equal eighty quarter-pound burgers with sixty-four glasses of wine.

THE SPARTAN DIET

The Spartans were warriors who stayed tough with extreme workouts and a punishing diet. Their dinners centered around "black soup," made from a pig's blood and (according to one ancient writer) every part of its body. But don't worry if that sounds grim. Reportedly, Spartans could vary the recipe using frogs, horses, goats, and other animals.

Meduso's Best PIGS FEET

> Eat just enough to keep you tough.

> When your leader isn't looking, eat like Milo of Croton.

Dinner's ready, honey!

Pottery from the Sparta area, made in about 570-560 BC

THIS FEAST IS A JOKE

Ancient Roman feasts were the wildest and most wasteful of all time.

When an emperor served flamingo tongues at a feast, he proved that he owned hundreds of the world's most beautiful birds and could waste them just for their tongues.

When living birds flew out of roasted pigs, his party stunts looked like magic.

One emperor supposedly served six hundred ostrich heads at a dinner, so guests could enjoy the bite-sized brains inside. While the rich ate ostrich brains in decayed fish juice, regular people had to settle for boring food like bread and olives.

GUESS WHO I AM

My rosy feathers give me my name,
But my tongue's tasty to gluttons.
What if my tongue turned talkative?

(Ancient Roman poem translated from Latin by James and Jenny Solheim)

Answer: a flamingo

20

FEAST DAY HIJINKS

Roman emperors sometimes entertained themselves with cruel pranks. One supposedly locked his guests in his feast hall with pet lions, bears, and leopards, without mentioning that they were tame.

Even worse, he served dinner.

ACTUAL RECIPES FROM ROMAN FEASTS

Help! I saw the food!

STUFFED DORMOUSE*

Pound fine-chopped pork and all of the dormouse's leg meat with pepper, nuts, laser root, and rotten-fish sauce. Stuff this mix into the dormouse and sew it shut. Place it on a tile and bake it in the oven or cook it in a roaster.

*A dormouse is an animal like a small squirrel that lives in and near Europe.

SCRAMBLED BRAINS AND CUCUMBERS

Cook peeled cucumbers with boiled brains, cumin, a little honey, celery seed, rotten-fish sauce, and oil. Thicken with eggs. Sprinkle with pepper and dish it out!

PART THREE

THE MIDDLE AGES

About AD 500 to about the fifteenth century

MYSTERY MEATS FOR MERRY MOUTHS

In olden times, a royal feast wasn't just a fancy meal. It was a show of power.

To make sure everyone recognized that power, kings became history students. When they learned that Roman emperors ate peacocks and wild pigs (called boars) at their feasts, England's kings did, too, over a thousand years later.

Usually they began a banquet with a roasted boar's head and moved on to extravagant dishes such as pies full of live eels or birds.

I sure hope kings get to eat cupcakes. Or I'm getting a new job.

It's twenty-four against one, buddy. I DARE you to come in and take us on.

HOW TO MAKE A JOKE PIE FULL OF LIVE BIRDS

According to a recipe from 1559:

First, make a piecrust with a hole in the bottom.
Fill it with flour to hold up the top crust. Add the top crust and bake.
Empty the flour out through the hole and stick live birds inside.
When cutting open the pie, let the birds fly out.
Then serve real pies so the guests won't feel cheated.

The famous poem based on this joke goes back centuries, but the dish is much older.

Sing a song of sixpence,
A pocket full of rye,
Four and twenty blackbirds,
Baked in a pie.

When the pie was opened
The birds began to sing;
Wasn't that a dainty dish
To set before the king?

EVEN BETTER THAN THE ROMANS

Europe's chefs had to outdo history's most creative and exotic feasts to prove their leaders the greatest of all time.

Here's just one lovely dish from surviving royal cookbooks: cow palates.

The dish swam with cow lips, cow noses, and the roofs of cows' mouths, along with rooster combs, animal glands, pickled flower buds, and more.

I love the special green sauce that comes with these cow noses!

Cow noses were in Martha Washington's cookbook, too!

The first US president, famous for his excellent dinners for guests →

WORMY STEAKS AND FIRE-BREATHING PEACOCKS

A fire-breathing peacock for dinner? No way!

Yes! Way!

To serve a fire-breathing peacock that people could actually eat, cooks carefully peeled the skin off a dead peacock with the feathers still attached. Then they baked the peacock and put the skin, feathers, and huge tail back on.

Last of all, they stuffed its beak with a cotton ball soaked in camphor (waxy crystals from the camphor tree) and lit the ball on fire. Then the peacock would "breathe fire for a long time," as the recipe said.

TIME-SAVING TIP
From Italy's finest medieval chefs

Leave the head, tail, and legs attached to the peacock's skin while removing it. When coaxing the feathered skin back onto the roasted bird, these parts will pop right into place.

SURE, YOU CAN STAY FOR DINNER

One cook in the Middle Ages came up with this way to scare away *smell-feasts*, people who "coincidentally" showed up at good-smelling meals hoping to be invited in to eat.

It's slang from the Middle Ages!

TO MAKE MEAT LOOK BLOODY AND WORMY AND SCARE AWAY SMELL-FEASTS
A recipe from merry old England

Boil rabbit's blood, dry it, and powder it.
Cast the powder onto boiled meat.
The heat and moisture will melt the powder
and make the meat look all bloody.
Cut small harp strings and drape them on the meat.
The heat will make them squirm like worms.*

*This only works with old-time harp strings, spun from cat guts!

THE MIDDLE AGES MAKE ME SICK

Most medicine in the Middle Ages didn't cure anything. From Asia to Europe to Africa, healers claimed all kinds of food had amazing powers.

But in a world where most people went hungry, even fried cockroaches and tiger eyeballs meant better nutrition—and maybe even accidentally better health.

> Take two tiger brains each morning and your laziness will clear right up.

	FOOD PRESCRIBED	ILLNESS CURED
EUROPE	Jelly made from whale guts	Liver and lung problems
	Powdered centipede in milk	Lockjaw and liver disease
	Hammered hamster liver soup	Skin or gland swelling
	Powdered whale heart in water	Heart trouble
	Whale eyelids in hot wine	Swollen or sore joints
	Crushed unicorn horn (narwhal tooth)	Poisoning
ASIA	Tiger brains	Laziness and zits
	Tiger eyeballs	Seizures and malaria
	Twice-fried cockroaches	Heart problems
	Bat poop	Blindness
	Flying squirrel poop	Malnutrition and snakebites
	Silkworm powder in ginger juice	Typhus and stomach problems
	Crushed dragon teeth and bones*	Insanely running around for no reason

*Actually from dug-up prehistoric animals, including mammoths

> For moderate to severe cobra bites, my doctor recommends Old World Brand Flying Squirrel Poop.

Bangkok, Thailand:
Giant water bugs

WHERE THE BARGAINS NEVER STOP

Many of today's historic food markets go back hundreds or even thousands of years. These are just a few of the markets and the traditional treats you can still buy at them. Each bite is a mouthful of history.

Santiago, Chile:
Warm donkey milk squeezed from the donkey as you watch

Tsukiji fish market in Tokyo: Tuna eyeballs as big as tennis balls

SALE!
GATOR SURPRISE!

Seoul, South Korea:
Live octopi

French Market in New Orleans:
Really fresh alligator meat

Huancayo, Peru:
Dried frogs

Durban, South Africa:
Smileys (sheep heads)

Kashgar, China:
Live scorpions

Bergen, Norway:
Smoked eel

Melbourne, Australia:
Kangaroo meat

PART FOUR

THE WORLD LEARNS WHAT OTHERS EAT

The end of the Middle Ages to Lewis and Clark (About 1500-1800s)

SAVE SOME CUCKOO BRAINS FOR ME
China, 1720

Being an emperor was hazardous. So China's ruler had an idea. To get competing parts of his empire to work together, he threw a feast to celebrate each region's foods.

The Manchu-Han Imperial Feast became a tradition. In this yearly event, top chefs showed off rare and tantalizing foods from all over China.

With at least 108 dishes and probably many more, the feast lasted for days.

Manchu-Han Feast Sampler

Rhino tails

Ape lips

Fish air bladders

Tiger tails

Monkey head mushrooms

Donkey nest fungus

Shark fins

Golden Eyes and Burning Brain
(a sculpture made of soybeans
with chicken, duck, and cuckoo brains)

Goat brains

HEART HEALTHY

The world has eaten snakes and drunk their blood for thousands of years.

In Vietnam, one living tradition is to swallow a cobra's beating heart whole after gulping its blood. Discerning diners feel its tickly twitch all the way down. They can even feel it fluttering in their stomachs.

Ah-ah-ah-CHOOOO!

Kootchie kootchie koo

esophagus

stomach

pancreas

intestines

appendix

PEE-YOO, THAT STINKS! SO LET'S EAT IT!
Europe and Asia from the Middle Ages to today

The musk deer has a gland that squirts greasy stuff called *musk* on trees. One drop of it can stink up the air for blocks.

Of course, somebody said, "Let's try it in our food!"

In an era of hair piled to the ceiling and dresses so wide their wearers often couldn't sit, Europeans went to excess with food, too. They paid big money to bring musk from Tibet to use in candy and perfume, often fooled by fake musk. One trader said that if you sniff musk up close and your nose bleeds, it's real. Nobody could cheat *him*.

I'll choose . . .

THIS pile!

Musk was— and is—more costly than gold.

HELP! CANDY ATTACK!

An English candy recipe from Robert May's 1660 book *The Accomplisht Cook* contained musk, *ambergris* (waxy chunks from whale poop), and *civet*. Animals called palm civets (similar to skunks) spray civet at their enemies.

Take that, you scoundrel!

NOSE WARNING

STINKS SO GOOD

When mammoth meat got moldy, people had to eat it anyway to survive.

But over the centuries, people learned to like the new experiences that stinkiness brought to their food. Still, there are many foods we need two hands to eat—one to hold the food and one to hold our noses.

> Quick! We've got to get him out of here! He might like this stuff better than our brussels sprouts!

P.U. ALERT

NOSE CLAMPS REQUIRED 🟢 **KEEP OUT OF FACE**

NOT APPROVED FOR GROWNUPS

DO NOT INHALE ☠

Durian (Southeast Asia)
A football-sized fruit sometimes banned for its odor, it comes in hundreds of varieties whose different degrees of flavor send durian devotees on a lifelong quest.

Funazushi (Japan) Let a dead goldfish ripen for a year using a recipe passed down since 1619, and you'll get a smell like the world's oldest sock but a taste with a gourmet zing.

Hongeo-hoe (Korea)
Left in hay to decay, this relative of stingrays smells like a toilet because it pees through its skin. But those who can get past the eye-blistering fumes learn to love the taste beneath.

Surströmming (Sweden)
These cans of decayed fish give off so much stinky gas that one exploded in a fire and flew across a bay.

Stinking toe fruit (Mexico, Central and South America)
Looks and smells like a giant toe unwashed for weeks, but its pulp is perfect in smoothies and Brazilian cookies called *broinhas*.

ACORNS AND CRITTERS
United States and Britain, ancient times to the twentieth century

Humans can't eat acorns straight off the tree. They taste nasty and make people sick.

Ancient innovators in California's Hoopa Valley Tribe figured out how to make acorns into food. One way is to dry them for a year, crack off the shells, pound the inner nuts into a powder, and spend at least a day washing out the nastiness. That turns toxic acorns into gourmet cuisine.

Acorn bread tastes great, acorns are free, and the bread only takes a year to make!

Mom, are the acorn cookies done yet?

I already told you—they'll be done in 364 days, 23 hours, and 59 minutes. Don't be so impatient!

BREAKFAST-TIME BRAVERY

American heroes from Sacagawea to Eisenhower knew how to enjoy a good squirrel.

Abraham Lincoln

Sacagawea

James Garfield

Dwight Eisenhower

POLITE TO STRANGERS

From 1804 to 1806, Meriwether Lewis and William Clark explored the American West. They survived the wilderness with the help of Native Americans who gave them food, guidance, and other help.

Lewis and Clark's Recorded Menu, April 9 to April 27, 1805

Beaver, beaver tail, deer, deer liver, elk, buffalo, buffalo calves, buffalo tongue, antelope, white rabbit, muskrat, otter, grizzly bear, goose, goose eggs, bald eagles, swan

"The dog. . . has become a favorite food. . . I prefer it to lean venison or elk, and [it] is very far superior to the horse . . . ."

ALL-NATURAL INGREDIENTS

Squirrel meat is deliciously nutty, abundant, and free. Native Americans made use of every part by pounding the critters and eating the pulp, bones and all. Mountain people especially liked the brains. Up into the late twentieth century, cookbooks including *Joy of Cooking* explained how to skin and stew squirrels. Why aren't we all making use of this great natural resource that was a favorite of Queen Victoria?

From homemade to the factory to the future

KETCHUP THROUGH THE CENTURIES

Ketchup first appeared in China before 1700, where the word meant "pickled fish juice." It was a way to turn rotting seafood into a pungent sauce. It contained no tomatoes.

> And if you grow up to be decayed like me, you can be ketchup!

> YAY!

Clap clap clap

Sailors brought ketchup to Europe. After its first appearance in a popular 1727 cookbook, ketchup recipes flooded England and America.

First Lady Martha Washington's recipes included ketchup made from pickled oysters. Author Jane Austen reportedly loved ketchup made of unripe walnuts mashed for days and fermented for a year. Americans made ketchup out of anything from anchovies to decayed mushrooms.

> Ketchup . . . ketchup . . . must have ketchup.

The first known ketchup recipes with tomatoes came in 1812. (Before then, many people thought tomatoes were poisonous.) As the century went on, commercial ketchup makers began adding coal tar, acid, formaldehyde, and other chemicals to keep it pretty.

I'm returning this ketchup because it has **TOMATO LIQUIDS** in it! Don't you know tomatoes are deadly?

In 1902, the US government began a process that led to banning poisonous chemicals in food—but not mold and fly larvae, also known as maggots.

Thank *goodness* they didn't ban our babies, my darling!

Today the internet is alive with creative ketchups, including ones like those from George Washington's time. But the US government's official rules still allow more mold than tomatoes in ketchup—and nutritious mashed maggots that once lived in the tomatoes!

Hmm . . . caterpillar ketchup? Shoe ketchup? Triple-foaming mustard ketchup? Which new product will make me a ketchup zillionaire?

I know! A revolutionary new ketchup made out of rotten fish!

JELL-O FREE-FOR-ALL!

Gelatin was originally a food for the rich—edible artworks jiggling at medieval Europe's royal feasts. It took days to make, starting with bones, skin, and gristle of pigs and cows. Only people with servants had time for it.

But inventor and eventual presidential candidate Peter Cooper had an idea: the world's first "just add hot water" gelatin. He owned a glue factory, and gelatin was made of the same thing as his glue. Now a cook wouldn't need to dismantle an animal and toil for days to put a stunning royal dish on the table.

Then, in 1897, cough-syrup makers Pearle and May Wait added colors, flavors, and sugar. May named it Jell-O. Now every step of gelatin preparation was easy. A Jell-O war began, with cooks across America trying to outdo each other's gourmet creations.

These are all actual recipes from the Jell-O mania that began in 1904 and lasted for decades.

SpaghettiOs and wieners in Jell-O (a variant of a 1957 recipe, "Hot Dog and Macaroni Aspic")

Cow tongue in Jell-O (1915)

Peter Cooper, quick gelatin inventor

Spam, pickles, ripe olives, and vinegar in Jell-O (1952)

Perfection salad: carrots, celery, vinegar, and cabbage in Jell-O (1904). It won third place in a recipe contest and became so popular that it sparked a century of Jell-O creativity.

THE MAGIC OF JELL-O

To kids in *1900*, Jell-O seemed like a magic powder that could turn a bowl of water into a gleaming jiggle blob. Jell-O was science, it was fun, it was cheap, and it was the art supply for a new burst of kitchen creativity. It became a leader in the new world of factory-made food.

Salmon, peas, and cucumbers in lemon Jell-O (1958)

Canned tuna, Jell-O, and enough mayonnaise to turn it white (1955)

A fake pineapple made of Jell-O, olives, mayo, and liver sausage (1953)

Liver, canned green beans, and artificial sweetener whipped into Jell-O (1974)

REALLY FAST FOOD:
FIFTY MILLION MILES PER HOUR TO THE STARS

A starship averaging fifty million miles an hour would take more than fifty years to get to the closest star. So any ship to the stars will need to recycle its food—and especially its water.

Luckily, the International Space Station already filters the harmful stuff out of pee to make a mouthwatering drink. Even the lab rats contribute—and the result is much cleaner than water we drink on Earth.

THIS SPACESHIP NEEDS MORE SUGAR

Food is heavy, but spaceships have to stay light to blast into space. So a rocket scientist named Sidney Schwartz made super-strong boards out of food. Instead of carrying tons of food whose weight would slow them down, astronauts could eat parts of the ship after a little soaking and cooking.

The boards held bolts well and didn't splinter when sawed. And Sidney ate them. But the space program has not used his recipe yet, missing out on a unique flavor.

Without gravity, liquids float in the air as jiggly balls.

Um, I think this water recycling system might need a little work.

B

BANANA-FLAVORED SPACECRAFT BOARDS
An Experimental Recipe from NASA's Sidney Schwartz

Ingredients: flour, corn starch, powdered milk, banana flakes, corn grits.

Directions: Combine ingredients. Heat to 400 degrees Fahrenheit and press into panels with three thousand pounds of pressure.

Uses: cabinets, shelves, siding, spacecraft walls, breakfast cereal.

YOU CRASH YOUR TIME-TRAVELING BIKE

. . . and a girl yells, "The woolly mammoth burgers are done!"

You just stare. "Mammoths? But this is the future!"

She slides a burger onto a plate. "What century are you from? Mammoth meat comes from the meat printer, obviously, not animals. Mammoths live in the zoo."

Her mom hurries over. "Don't forget to eat dessert before dinner!" She hands you a cookie. "I printed these from wild stink bugs and our own recycled sewage. You can have a stink bug burger, too, if you catch them yourself."

With a careful nibble, you let the crumbs rest on your tongue before risking a swallow. Buttery, crisp, plus a flavor like . . . what? Toad gas. The fumes from a car-flattened toad on a hot day.

You grab your bike.

You are flying out of here. Pedaling back to your own time as fast as you can. (To tell your friends.)

Because that was the best cookie you ever tasted!

More Reading and Doing
Food Fun from Prehistory to the Future

Solheim, James. *It's Disgusting—and We Ate It!* New York: Simon & Schuster, 1998.

Cole, Adam, et al. *The Time Traveler's Cookbook: Meat-Lover's Edition.* NPR, 2012. https://media.npr.org/news/graphics/2012/06/the-time-travellers-meat-lovers-cookbook.pdf

Gordon, David George. *The Eat-a-Bug Cookbook.* Berkeley: Ten Speed Press, 2013.

Ramos-Elorduy, Julieta, and Peter Menzel. *Creepy Crawly Cuisine: The Gourmet Guide to Edible Insects.* Rochester, VT: Park Street Press 1998.

Gifford, Clive. *Food and Cooking in Ancient Rome/Ancient Egypt/Ancient Greece* (series). New York: PowerKids Press.

You Wouldn't Want to Be . . . (series). Dozens of books about the difficulties of life in different historical periods, covering everything from food to travel to customs. Brighton: Book House.

Carson, Laurie. *Hands-On History* (series). Books about life in different time periods, with fun actitivies. Chicago: Chicago Review Press.

Elliott, Lynne. *Food and Feasts in the Middle Ages.* New York: Crabtree Publishing Company, 2004.

Gunderson, Mary. *Exploring History Through Simple Recipes* (series). Mankato, MN: Blue Earth Books.

Brown, Sally, and Kate Morris. *The World in My Kitchen: Global Recipes for Kids to Discover and Cook.* London: Nourish, 2016.

McLeod Stephen A., editor. *Dining with the Washingtons.* Mount Vernon, VA: Mount Vernon Ladies' Association, 2011.

Clarkson, Janet. *Menus from History: Historic Meals and Recipes for Every Day of the Year.* Santa Barbara, California: Greenwood Press/ABC-CLIO, 2009.

Aki, Evi. *Flavors of Africa: Discover Authentic Family Recipes from All Over the Continent.* Salem, MA: Page Street Publishing, 2018.

Galimberti, Gabriele. *In Her Kitchen: Stories and Recipes from Grandmas Around the World.* New York: Clarkson Potter, 2014.

Bourland, Charles T., and Gregory L. Vogt. *The Astronaut's Cookbook.* New York: Springer, 2010.

The Incredibly Disgusting Story series (about modern processed foods). New York: Rosen Central.

Select Bibliography

Adamson, Melitta Weiss. *Food in Medieval Times: Food Through History.* Westport, CT: Greenwood, 2004.

Aveling, E. M. and C. Heron. "Chewing tar in the early Holocene: an archaeological and ethnographic evaluation." *Antiquity* 73 (281): 579–584. September 1, 1999.

Backwell, Lucinda R. and Francesco d'Errico. "Evidence of termite foraging by Swartkrans early hominids." *Proceedings of the National Academy of Sciences of the United States Of America* 98 (4): 1358–1363. February 13, 2001.

Bhagwandin, Adhil, Mark Haagensen, and Paul R. Manger. "The brain of the black (*Diceros bicornis*) and white (*Ceratotherium simum*) African rhinoceroses: morphology and volumetrics from magnetic resonance imaging." *Frontiers in Neuroanatomy* 11:74, 2017.

Borschberg, Peter. "The European musk trade with Asia in the early Modern Period." *The Heritage Journal* 1 (1): 1–12. 2004.

Brugère, Alexis, Laure Fontana, and M. Oliva. "Mammoth procurement and exploitation at Milovice (Czech Republic): new data for the Moravian Gravettian." *Proceedings of the XVth UISPP Congress*, Session C61, 42: 45–69. 2009.

Bryan, Cyril P., ed. *The Papyrus Ebers.* London: Geoffery Bles, 1930.

Callaway, Ewen. "Neanderthal tooth plaque hints at meals—and kisses." *Nature* 543 (7644): 163. March 8, 2017.

Clark, Katherine A., Salima Ikram, and Richard P. Evershed. "Organic chemistry of balms used in the preparation of pharaonic meat mummies." *Proceedings of the National Academy of Sciences of the United States of America.* 110 (51): 20392–20395. November 18, 2013.

Cooper, Peter. "Improvement in the preparation of portable gelatine." Arlington, VA: U.S. Patent Office. Patent No. 4,084, dated June 20, 1845.

Dawson, Warren R. "The mouse in Egyptian and later medicine." *The Journal of Egyptian Archaeology* 10 (2): 83-86, 1924.

Dharmananda, Subhuti. "Dragon bones and teeth." Institute for Traditional Medicine, Portland, Oregon. http://www.itmonline.org/arts/dragonbone.htm

Elias, Scott. *Advances in Quaternary Entomology.* Amsterdam: Elsevier, 2010.

Englund, Robert K. "There's a rat in my soup!" *Altorientalishe Forschungen* 22: 37–55. 1995.

Ferraro, Joseph V., et al. "Earliest archaeological evidence of persistent hominin carnivory." *PLoS One* 8 (4): e62174. April 25, 2013.

Fombong, Forkwa and John Kinyuru. "Termites as food in Africa." Chapter from *Termites and Sustainable Management*, edited by Md Aslam Khan and Wasim Ahmad. Cham, Switzerland: Springer, 2018. 10.1007/978-3-319-72110-1_11.

Food Defect Levels. U.S. Food and Drug Administration, March 24, 2021.

Hardy, Karen, et al. "Diet and environment 1.2 million years ago revealed through analysis of dental calculus from Europe's oldest hominin at Sima del Elefante, Spain." *The Science of Nature* 104 (2): February 2017. https://doi.org/10.1007/s00114-016-1420-x

Heimpel, Wolfgang. *Letters to the King of Mari.* Winona Lake, IN: Eisenbrauns, 2003.

Hendy, Jessica, et al. "Proteomic evidence of dietary sources in ancient dental calculus." *Proceedings of the Royal Society B* 285: 20180977. July 18, 2018. http://dx.doi.org/10.1098/rspb.2018.0977

Hernek, Robert, and Bengt Nordqvist. "Världens äldsta tuggummi?" Stockholm: Riksantikvarieämbetet, 1995.

Ingicco, T., et al., "Earliest known hominin activity in the Philippines by 709 thousand years ago," *Nature* 557: 233–237. May 2, 2018.

Jensen, T.Z.T., et al. "A 5700-year-old human genome and oral microbiome from chewed birch pitch." *Nature Communications* 10 (1): 5520, 2019.

Johnson, Keith L., et al. "A tick from a prehistoric Arizona coprolite" (2008). *Papers in Natural Resources* 59. http://digitalcommons.unl.edu/natrespapers/59.

Kharlamova, Anastasia, et al. "Preliminary analyses of brain gross morphology of the woolly mammoth, *Mammuthus primigenius*, from Yakutia, Russia." Supplement to the online *Journal of Vertebrate Paleontology*, p. 153A, 2013.

Kjellström, Anna, et al. "Capturing the moment: chewing today and 10,000 years ago." *AmS-Skrifter* 23: 53–61. 2010.

Lo, Vivian. *Medieval Chinese Medicine: the Dunhuang Medical Manuscripts.* London, New York: RoutledgeCurzon, 2005.

Machamer, Peter, Marcello Pera, and Aristides Baltas, eds. *Scientific Controversies: Philosophical and Historical Perspectives.* New York, Oxford: Oxford University Press, 2000.

Magie, David, translator. *Historia Augusta*, Vol. II. Cambridge, MA: Harvard University Press, 2014.

Maixner, Frank, et al., "The Iceman's last meal consisted of fat, wild meat, and cereals." *Current Biology* 28 (14): 2348-2355, 2018. July 23, 2018.

Mark, Joshua J. "The banquet stele of Ashurnasirpal II." *The Ancient History Encyclopedia*, 17 July 2014. https://www.ancient.eu/article/730/the-banquet-stele-of-ashurnasirpal-ii

Marshall, Amadine. "About the efficacy of eating a cooked mouse." *Ancient Egypt Magazine* 88, 15 (4): 40–42, 2015.

Mathews, Jennifer P. *Chicle: the Chewing Gum of the Americas, from the Ancient Maya to William Wrigley.* Tucson: University of Arizona Press, 2009.

May, Robert. *The Accomplisht Cook, or the Art and Mystery of Cookery.* Gloucester, UK: Dodo Press, 2010, reprinted from 1660 book.

McCouat, Philip. "The life and death of Mummy Brown." *The Journal of Art in Society.* http://www.artinsociety.com/the-life-and-death-of-mummy-brown.html

McPherron, Shannon P., et al. "Evidence for stone-tool-assisted consumption of animal tissues before 3.39 million years ago at Dikika, Ethiopia." *Nature* 466: 857–860. August 12, 2010.

Nguyen, Luke. *My Vietnam: Stories and Recipes.* Guilford, CT: Lyons Press, 2009.

Nowell, April, C., et al. "Middle Pleistocene subsistence in the Azraq Oasis, Jordan: protein residue and other proxies." *Journal of Archaeological Science* 72: 36–44. July 26, 2016.

Revedin, Anna, et al. "Thirty-thousand-year-old evidence of plant food processing." *Proceedings of the National Academy of Sciences of the United States of America* 107 (44): 18815–18819. November 2, 2010.

Reynolds, Frances. "Food and drink in Babylonia." From Leick, Gwendolyn, editor, *The Babylonian World,* 171–184. New York: Routledge, 2007.

Roach, Mary. *Packing for Mars: The Curious Science of Life in the Void.* New York: W.W. Norton, 2010.

Scully, Terence. *Cuoco Napoletano. The Neapolitan Recipe Collection.* Ann Arbor: The University of Michigan Press, 2000.

Smith, Andrew F. *Pure Ketchup: A History of America's National Condiment, with Recipes.* Columbia, S.C.: University of South Carolina Press, 1996.

Smith, Eliza. *The Compleat Housewife.* London: J. and J. Pemberton, 1739.

Sommerfeld, Samantha. "The Hoopa Valley tribe: the importance of acorns." *Native American Forestry.* 2008. https://www.uwsp.edu/forestry/StuJournals/Pages/NA/sommerfeld.aspx

Steele, Teresa E. "A unique hominin menu dated to 1.95 million years ago." *Proceedings of the National Academy of Sciences of the United States of America* 107 (24): 10771–10772, 2010.

Toussaint-Samat, Maguelonne. *A History of Food.* Malden, MA: Wiley-Blackwell, 2008.

von Bingen, Hildegard. *Hildegard von Bingen's Physica.* Priscilla Throop, translator. Rochester, VT: Healing Arts Press, 1998.

Wade, Lizzie. "How Egyptian mummies took food to the afterlife." *Wired.* November 19, 2013. https://www.wired.com/2013/11/egyptian-mummies-afterlife-diet

Wei-Haas, Maya. "5,300 years ago, Ötzi the Iceman died. Now we know his last meal." *National Geographic.* July 12, 2018. https://www.nationalgeographic.com/science/2018/07/news-otzi-iceman-food-DNA-diet-meat-fat

Wescott, David, editor. *Primitive Technology II: Ancestral Skill.* Salt Lake City: Gibbs Smith, 2001.

Williams, A.R. "Packing food for the hereafter in ancient Egypt." *National Geographic.* April 5, 2015. https://www.nationalgeographic.com/culture/article/packing-food-for-the-hereafter-in-ancient-egypt

Wrangham, Richard. *Catching Fire: How Cooking Made Us Human.* New York: Basic Books, 2009.

Wyman, Carolyn. *Jell-O: A Biography.* San Diego: Harcourt, 2001.

"You Can Drill It, Make Things. . . Even Have It for Breakfast." *Grumman Plane News,* April 26, 1963.

Special thanks to Robert K. Englund, Allison Thomason, Thomas Ingicco, Sherwin Gormly, Larry Feliu, Astrid Hilger Bennett, Karl Reinhard, Ruth Clark, Hannes Schroeder, Anastasia Kharlamova, Sergey Saveliev, Evgeny Maschenko, Joumana Accad, April Nowell, Sami Viljanmaa, Libby Rosemeier, Theis Jensen, Marie Rayner, Renea Wayna, Lynne Belluscio, and Meghan Christine Cassidy.

Image Credits

All images are by James Solheim, except those available by public domain, by permission, through a Creative Commons license, through unsplash.com/license, or through pexels.com/photo-license. For more detailed information, visit jamessolheim.com/licenses.html.

COVER: George Washington by Gilbert Stuart and Rembrandt Peale. Hand by Charles Peale Polk. Other hand by Gilbert Stuart. Arm and body by Daniel John Pound. Lower legs by Nargeot. Eels by Greg Thompson for the U.S. Fish and Wildlife Service. Apple pie by Andrea Hamilton. Grasshopper by Claudia Peters. Squirrel by Guy Leroux. Cricket parts by Gail Hampshire. Buzz Aldrin by Neil Armstrong for NASA. Mammoth by Charles R. Knight. **ENDPAPERS:** Nefertiti, attributed to Thutmose in about 1345 BC, photographed by icelight. Shakespeare by John Taylor. Eyes by LeuschteLampe. Hand holding mouse by Niek Verlaan. Rhino brain by Paul R. Manger. Bug legs by Frank Vassen. S'mores by Evan-Amos. Tarantula from "Insects Unlocked" by Alejandro Santillan and Lexi Roberts. Pie mouse by Robert Owen Wahl. Eel by Greg Thompson for the U.S. Fish and Wildlife Service. Mammoth by Charles R. Knight. Liver Jell-O by RetroRuth (Ruth Clark), midcenturymenu.com. Oyster shell by Javier Lastras. Oyster by Priscilla Yuen. Fish eyeballs by Southeast Fisheries Science Center Pascagoula Laboratory, Collection of Brandi Noble. Scorpions by Rudy Herman. Tortillas by LI1324. Starfish by Ven. Rangama Chandawimala Thero. Camel meat by Krista Garcia, goodiesfirst.com. **COPYRIGHT/TITLE/CONTENTS PAGES:** Fire by Chris Rhoads. Branch by Zach Reiner. Brain from *Das menschliche Gehirn* by R.A. Pfeifer, Wellcome Collection. Einstein by Acme Newspictures. Clothes by Nick Karvounis. Einstein's hands by Niek Verlaan. Grasshopper by Elegance Thika. Green eye by Heikki Siltala, heikkisiltala.com. Orange eye by U.S. Fish and Wildlife Service. Brownish eyes by LeuschteLampe. Insect grub by Grey Geezer. Vapor eyes by Rembrandt van Rijn. Shark by Timothy Knepp, U.S. Fish and Wildlife Service, USFWS National Digital Library. **PAGE 2:** Mom and boy from *Saturday Evening Post*, April 12, 1952, scanned by Justin Solheim. Mammoth photo by Evgeny Maschenko, by permission. Mom's hand by Sergey Zolkin, modified. **PAGE 3:** Waring mixer from *Better Homes & Gardens*, November 1955, scanned by James Solheim. Rhino brain by Paul R. Manger. Stone tool by April Nowell. World-record Twinkie by Libby Rosemeier. **PAGE 5:** Drinking glass by FxJ. Foam by Stefan Grage. Sheep brain by Manimaran96. Dress frill by Malgorzata Smozewska. Horse heart by Jean de Saunier. Sky by Carsten Frenzl. **PAGE 6:** Fly by USDA.gov. Beetle by Roland Kuck. Flea by Andrei Savitsky. Louse by Janice Harney Carr, Center for Disease Control. Cockroach by Dirk (Beeki®) Schumacher. Iguana skin by Brian Gratwicke. Grasshopper by Egor Kamelev. Einstein by Orren Jack Turner, modified by PM Poon and Dantadd. Brain from Wellcome Collection. First Confirmation of a Neutral Current Interaction © 1973–2020 CERN. **PAGE 7:** Mastodon by Charles R. Knight from an 1897 painting. Termites by Alfredo Flores, USDA Forest Service. Taco by Renee Comet, National Cancer Institute. **PAGE 8:** Jimmy Carter's smile by Karl Schumacher © White House. Top cheese eye by Amanda Dalbjörn. Lower eye by LeuschteLampe. Moonworts by Jason Hollinger. Cattail by AnRo0002. Cattail by Ryan. Smartweed by Harry Rose. Cutworms by USGS Bee Inventory and Monitoring Lab. Walt Whitman by Mathew Brady, from U.S. National Archives and Records Administration. Moon by NASA/JPL-Caltech. Pseudoscorpion by Marshal Hedin. Orange eye by Woodwalker. Green eye by Jeffrey Buchbinder. Ponytail by deerstop. Gray rocks by icelight. **PAGE 9:** Teosinte by Hugh Iltis. Prehistoric popcorn by Tom Dillehay. Buffalo Bill's mustache by Henry Van der Weyde. Jackie Onassis's hair by Robert Knudsen, JFK Library and Museum. Yellow suit by Mariya Georgiva. Cabbage moth caterpillars by David Short. **PAGE 10:** Stone in glasses by Emery Muhozi. Gray gum by Theis Jensen. Tan gum by Sami Viljanmaa, Kierikki Stone Age Centre. Black gum by Natalija Kashuba. Pink bubble by Gisela Merkuur, gisela-fotografie.nl. **PAGE 11:** Pre-Columbian pot by unknown Mexican artist about 1200–1521, photographed by Sailko. Mastic gum by Joumana Accad, tasteofbeirut.com. Alexander the Great by unknown ancient artist, photographed by Ángel M. Felicísimo. **PAGE 12:** Boris Karloff as the Mummy by Universal Pictures. Tut headdress underlayer photographed by Carsten Frenzl. **PAGE 13:** Mumia by Christoph Braun. Louvre mummy wraps photographed by jalvear. Mummy heads copyright © Merck, emdgroup.com. **PAGE 14:** Swimming pool by MCSAM. Naffur temple ruins by Jasmine N. Walthall, U.S. Army. **PAGE 15:** Hammurabi inscription from *A Guide to the Babylonian and Assyrian Antiquities* by Ernest Alfred Wallis Budge and Leonard William King, 1908. Mesopotamian recipe tablet from the Yale Babylonian Collection. **PAGE 16:** Pythagoras head by unknown artist (Roman copy of a Greek statue from first or second century BC), photo by Szilas. Baby carriage from cabinetmaker and furniture catalog circa 1886, from thegraphicsfairy.com. Green bean, black bean, and lima bean by Renee Comet for the National Cancer Institute. Discus thrower, Roman copy of a lost sculpture by Myron of Eleutherae, who lived about 480–440 BC in ancient Greece, photographed by Matthias Kabel. Hera, Roman copy of a lost sculpture by unknown Greek artist, circa third century BC, photographed by Marie-Lan Nguyen (Jastrow), from the Louvre. Eel by James Carson Brevoort, 1818–1887. Eyes by LeuschteLampe. **PAGE 17:** Marathon Boy by the School of Praxiteles, about 340–330 BCE, photographed by Jebulon. Fish by NOAA from fishwatch.gov. Athena from the Archaeological Museum of Piraeus (Athens), by Kephisodotos or Euphranor (fourth century BC) or an unknown artist, photographed by Giovanni Dall'Orto. Octopus by T. Tseng. **PAGE 18:** Cow from *Johnson's Household Book of Nature*, by Hugh Craig, 1880, in thegraphicsfairy.com. Poison ivy by BrolyO. **PAGE 19:** Temple at Olympia by Karta24. Pickle jar by Anne & Saturnino Miranda. Pigs' feet by Bryan Ledgard. Marble floor by MM. Mosaic floor from page 160 of *Architecture, Classic and Early Christian* by John Slater and T. Roger Smith, 1888. Pot from Sparta by the workshop of the Boreads Painter, the Metropolitan Museum of Art. Bornean bearded pig by Mike Prince. Dress by Jean Jacques François Lebarbier, from "A Spartan Woman Giving a Shield to Her Son" at the Portland Art Museum collection.

PAGE 20: Eyes by Gisela Merkuur, gisela-fotografie.nl. Robed statue photographed by Marie-Lan Nguyen (Jastrow). Heads photographed by Bibi Saint-Pol. Caesar Augustus photographed by Bradley Weber. **PAGE 21:** Statue head photo by Jastrow. Eyes by LeutscheLampe. Ostrich by Lourdes Alvarez Martinez. Wing by Jean van der Meulen, jeanvdmeulen.com. Hat by Frank K. **PAGE 22:** Still life by Floris van Dyck, 1610, from the Frans Hals Museum. Pie shell by Anna Tukhfatullina. Crust by fugzu. **PAGE 23:** Queen from www.wopc.co.uk/blogs/kenlodge. George Washington "Williamstown Portrait" by Gilbert Stuart and Rembrandt Peale. **PAGE 24:** Peacock tail by Scott Edmunds. **PAGE 25:** Charlemagne by Louis-Félix Amiel. Frying pan and marshmallow by Evan-Amos. Chapelle de Languidou rose window by Patrice78500. Bottom flame by Ludovic Bertron. Top flame by Arghya Banik. Earthworms by Saikiransunkoju. **PAGE 26:** Flying squirrel by unknown, from *Fauna Japonica*, published between 1833–1850. Pumpkin stems by Steve. Galaxy by NASA, ESA, The Hubble Heritage Team, and P. Knezek (WIYN). **PAGE 27:** Escaping couple from *Monster on the Campus* poster by Reynold Brown. Sky by Harshit Sharma. **PAGE 28:** Dragon's pigeon brain from *The New Student's Reference Work*. Monkey head mushrooms by Henk Monster. **PAGE 30:** Big hair from 1902 Sears, Roebuck & Co. Catalog, reprinted by Gramercy, 1993. Flowers and mouse by Willem van Aelst, about 1656, Google Art Project. Ivy by Sereja Ris. Ship by Willem van de Velde the Younger. Lace by Edny Fauskanger, photographed and adapted by James Solheim. P.T. Barnum by W. R. Howell, engraved by George E. Perine. **PAGE 31:** Eyes by LeuschteLampe. Biohazard symbol by CRW at clker.com. Lips by Azamat Zhanisov. Surströmming by MartinThoma. Hongeo-hoe by 자유로. Durian by EquatorialSky. Stinkin' toe fruit by Mauroguanandi. Funazushi by Yasuo Kida. **PAGE 32:** Lincoln by Alexander Gardner. James Garfield by Mathew Brady from Library of Congress. Hat by unknown, photographed by Daderot. Eisenhower by White House, Eisenhower Presidential Library. **PAGE 33:** Queen Victoria, copy of a painting by Franz Xaver Winterhalter. Queen's arm by Niek Verlaan. Squirrel by Marcelo Vaz. **PAGE 34:** Shrimp color by Toa Heftiba, heftiba.co.uk. Wig from a portrait of Marquis de Lücker, 1696–1772, by Louis Tocqué. **PAGE 35:** Fruit fly by Scott Bauer, USDA Agricultural Research Service, bugwood.org. Other fruit fly by Joseph Berger, bugwood.org. Gray gravestone by AnnaER. Grass by Janko Ferlic. Sky from NASA on the Commons. **PAGES 36–37:** Baby's plate from *Dainty Desserts for Dainty People*, Charles B. Knox Company, 1915. Spam Jell-O from *American Home*, July 1952, scanned by James Solheim. Teddy Roosevelt ® Library of Congress. Roosevelt's sleeve by Garry Tucker, U.S. Fish and Wildlife Service Southeast Region. Red Jell-O by Hugo Hercer. Napkin by monicore, facebook.com/enthusiastudio. Perfection salad by Marie Rayner, theenglishkitchen.blogspot.com. SpaghettiO Jell-O by Renea Wayna. Peter Cooper by Mathew Brady, U.S. National Archives and Records Administration. Pearle B. Wait from the Kraft Heinz Company. Tuna Jell-O from *Women's Day*, May 1955, scanned by James Solheim. Pineapple by Brian Sauls. Hearts by Meghan Christine Cassidy. Liver Jell-O and Yellow Jell-O by Ruth Clark, midcenturymenu.com. Acrobat from poster by Morris père et fils ® Library of Congress. Acrobat from 1887 poster in the Bibliothèque nationale de France. Baseball players by Gilbert Bacon, and bottom fairy by Achille Devéria, from the New York Public Library digital collection. Top fairies from thegraphicsfairy.com, by Alfred Edward Chalon and by unknown. May Wait by permission of Lynne Belluscio at the Jell-O Gallery. **PAGES 38–39:** Neil Armstrong, rocket thrusters, exhaust, Earth, moon surface, space shuttle wings, liquid globes (modified by James Solheim), and International Space Station Water Recovery System by NASA. Buzz Aldrin by Neil Armstrong. Restroom symbol by Ocal at clker.com. Spigot and mouse by Robert Owen Wahl. Glass cracks by Paul Barlow. Scientist and flask by George Hodan. Plastic wrap by Hans Braxmeier. **PAGE 40:** Burger top by Patrick Tomasso of Eaters Collective. Cookies by Whitney Wright. **PAGE 43:** Mammoth brain by Anastasia Kharlamova and Sergei Saveliev. **PAGE 47:** Carrot by Liz West. **ENDPAPERS:** Napoleon by Jacques-Louis. Lung from OpenStax College—Anatomy & Physiology, Connexions. Golden fish eye by incidencematrix. Lionfish eye by Michael Gäbler. Telstar by Thomson200. Moose snout by Denali National Park and Preserve. Queen Elizabeth attributed to William Segar. Ambergris by Wmpearl. Brain by Daniel Hack Tuke. Chicha by Tisquesusa. Neil Armstrong, sky, and rocket by NASA. John F. Kennedy by U.S. Navy, ® Library of Congress. Beetle by Christina Butler, inaturalist.org/people/skitterbug. **BACK COVER:** Jell-O by Hugo Hercer. Lincoln's face by Alexander Gardner. Mammoth by Charles R. Knight.

Index of Very Special Foods

Oh, no! My disguise didn't work!

Kangaroo pie
(snarfed down in ancient and
modern Australia)

Mopane worms
(giant moth caterpillars
savored in southern Africa
from prehistory to today)

Goldfish crackers
(over three thousand baked
each second worldwide,
ingredients including phosphate
rock dug from the ground)

Ahriche
(internal organs on a stick,
enjoyed in Morocco from
prehistory to today)

Edible clay dug from the ground
(folded into potato sauce
in South America from the
Inca Empire to today)

Cow brain sandwich
(wolfed down in Saint Louis,
1800s to Modern Times)

Casu marzu
(cheese containing live, jumping maggots,
eaten on the island of Sardinia
from ancient times to today)

Alligator tail
(stewed in ancient and
contemporary Americas)